Could You Leave The Light On?

Illustrations: Ann de Bode
Original title: *Mag het licht nog even ann?*
© Van In, Lier, 1995. Van In Publishers, Grote Markt 39,
2500 Lier, Belgium.
© in this edition Evans Brothers Limited 1997
(world English rights excluding the USA and Canada)
English text by Su Swallow

First published in paperback in 1999

First published in Great Britain by
Evans Brothers Limited
2A Portman Mansions
Chiltern Street
London W1M 1LE

Printed by KHL (Singapore)

0 237 52041 9

HELPING HANDS

COULD YOU LEAVE THE LIGHT ON?

ANN DE BODE AND RIEN BROERE

Evans Brothers Limited

'Be good!' says Mum.
And gives a few more instructions.
Yes, all right, thinks Naomi. Off you go, Mum.
The train wheels squeak as they start to turn.
The train moves off.
'Bye, see you soon!' cries Naomi.
A hand waves to her through the window.
Mum has gone.

3

Naomi is going to stay with her cousin, Caroline.
Together they lift Naomi's case on to the bed.
Auntie Julie is there, too.
'Wait a minute,' Naomi says.
'I've got something for you.'
She starts looking in her case.
On the top is Zebbie, her favourite cuddly toy.
She won't give her away, that's for sure!

But what has happened? No parcel!
Naomi rummages through her case,
and starts to get cross.
She starts flinging things out.
Zebbie flies up to the ceiling.
Then a book, and a comb.
And a torch. And all her clothes.
Some of them land on Caroline.

Naomi searches the bottom of her case.
She can feel something.
Rustly paper and a bow,
and then another packet.
One for her cousin and one for her aunt.
But which is which?
Mum did tell her, but she has forgotten.

'Oh look!' says Auntie Julie. 'My favourite chocolates.
That's very kind. Thank you.'
Caroline tears the paper off her present.
'Oh, some soap. Thank you!'
But she looks a bit disappointed.
Her mum smells the soap.
'Mmm, nice,' she says. 'Shall we swap?'
'Yes please!' says Caroline.

Auntie Julie makes some pancakes.
She makes a big pile.
There are pancakes with sugar and lemon,
and some with chocolate powder and
some with strawberry jam.
Naomi eats lots, even one that didn't turn out right.
'Oof,' she sighs. 'I'm full up.
I feel as fat as a balloon!'

8

'Can we go to bed now?' asks Caroline.
Auntie Julie can hardly believe her ears.
'You want to go to bed already?
It's much too early. Go and play for a bit.'
That's a pity. The two cousins would love to go to bed.
Not to sleep, of course. To have some fun.
But they have to wait for quite a while.

'Here comes a snake,' threatens Caroline.
'Huh,' says Naomi. 'You can't scare me.'
Caroline squeezes the tube of toothpaste very hard
and a long snake of paste wriggles out.
Naomi takes no notice.
She goes very quiet all of a sudden.
She is thinking about later, when she will be in the dark.
She is afraid of the dark. But she doesn't say so.

'Let's pretend we're camping,' says Caroline.
'It's night, and my bed is our tent.
It's very dark, and very hot in the tent.
Suddenly, a cow creeps into our tent.'
'A cow?' laughs Naomi.
She can't imagine a cow creeping about.
'If you don't like it,' says Caroline,
'you think of something.'

So the tent bed turns into a boat bed.
At first, it sails gently on a calm sea.
But then...oh dear! A storm blows up.
The boat tips and rolls and creaks.
'Help,' cries Naomi. 'We're sinking!
And there are sharks everywhere.
They'll eat us up!'

Now the bed is a plane.
The two cousins are heroes.
They are going to save people.
'Someone's in trouble down there,' cries Caroline.
They both jump out of the plane.
'Hey,' says Naomi. 'Now the plane
has no pilot!'
So they both leap back on to the bed.

The bed lands safely, in the middle of a circus.
'Look,' says Caroline, 'I'm an elephant.'
'You don't look much like an elephant,' says Naomi.
'Look on the wall,' says Caroline.
Her shadow makes the head and trunk.
'You're only half an elephant,' says Naomi.
She crawls under the covers and
together they make a whole elephant.

The two girls are acrobats.
They jump so high that
their heads nearly touch the light.
'That's enough, you two!'
It's Auntie Julie calling.
They hadn't heard her coming upstairs.
'Stop the noise or I shall separate you.'

'Stop pretending to be asleep,' says Caroline.
But Naomi isn't pretending to be asleep.
She is thinking, 'Soon I shall have to go to my own bed.
And I shall be all alone for the rest of the night.
I can't tell Caroline I'm afraid.
She'll make fun of me.
She's not afraid of anything!'

'Oi! Say something!'
Caroline nudges her cousin.
Naomi nudges back, quite hard.
Caroline yells and falls out of bed with a bump.
Angry footsteps climb the stairs.
'Quick, under the bed,' says Caroline.
Two half-legs appear.
'Now where are they?' mutters Auntie Julie.

'Come along, I'll take you to your room,' says Auntie Julie.
'Goodnight,' calls Caroline. 'See you in the morning.'
Naomi hangs her head.
'Cheer up, I'm not really cross with you,' says Auntie Julie.
Naomi knows that.
She is thinking about the strange bed in a strange room.
She is worried about the dark that is waiting.
She is very quiet.

She knew what would happen.
As soon as Auntie Julie closes the door,
it starts.
Naomi starts to feel afraid.
She slides down under the covers.
She holds Zebbie tight.
But she can see them already.
The monsters are coming to get her...

Perhaps they are under the bed.
'Go on, you have a look,' whispers Naomi,
and hangs Zebbie upside down to search.
Naomi holds her by the tail.
After a while she pulls her toy back into bed.
'Well?' asks Naomi. 'Did you see anything?'
Zebbie says nothing, but Naomi is not convinced.

Very, very slowly, Naomi opens her eyes.
Suddenly, her heart starts pounding.
Something is moving in the corner of the room!
She can see a shadow on the wall.
It's a monster with at least seven heads.
Fourteen claws reach out towards her.
Naomi hides behind Zebbie.

Naomi nearly screams.
In the other corner a black ghost hovers.
It stares at her with one bright eye
and pulls a nasty face.
Naomi thinks: 'They're coming to get me.
They'll take me to the cave of the night,
where it's always cold and morning
never comes.' She has never felt so afraid.

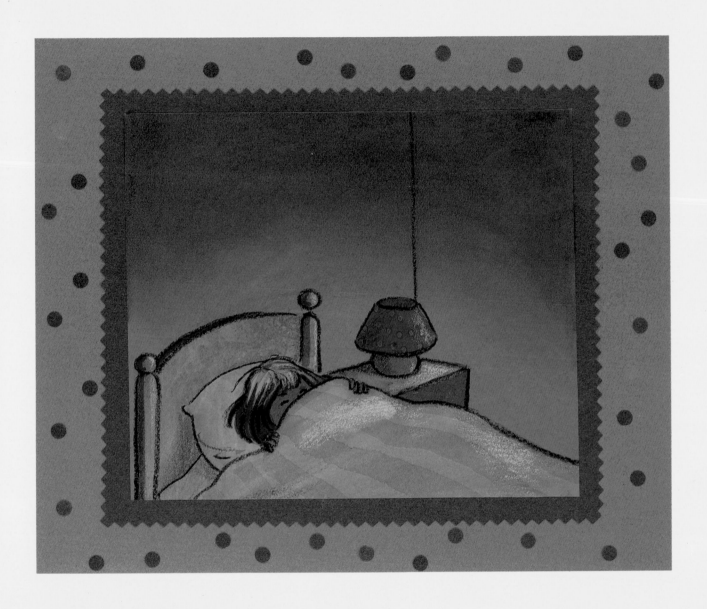

Naomi closes her eyes very tight.
So tight that she can see stars.
'If only I could be home again,' she says to herself.
'If only Mum could be here.
If I call Auntie Julie, Caroline will wake up
and make fun of me.'
Naomi wishes she were big and strong.

At last Naomi falls asleep.
But even in her sleep she isn't safe.
She has a scary dream about twenty sharks.
'No!' she cries, and half wakes up.
'I'm going to find Mum.'
She gets up, and wakes up properly.
'Where am I? This is not my room.'

Then Naomi remembers where she is.
At Auntie Julie's house. Of course.
She laughs at herself,
and climbs back into bed.
But what is that?
A stair creaks. Someone is coming!
Now what can she do? She sees her case.
She slips out of bed and creeps over to it.

Naomi feels about inside her case.
'Where have I put it?' she thinks.
'I know it's here somewhere.'
She looks over at the door. The handle is turning.
Slowly, the door opens.
Just then, Naomi finds her torch and switches it on.
It lights up her face.
'Aaah!' someone yells from the doorway. 'Help!'

Naomi recognises the voice of Auntie Julie.
'Help, a ghost!' cries Auntie Julie.
'I'm not a ghost, it's me, Auntie,' says Naomi.
Auntie Julie puts on the light.
'So it is,' she says, laughing nervously.
'I knew it was you all the time.'

The noise wakes Caroline.
The three of them sit on Auntie Julie's bed.
Auntie Julie tells them about her ghost.
And Naomi tells them how scared she had been.
'I saw a monster,' she says. 'And a ghost.'
Caroline laughs at her.
But Naomi doesn't mind.
She is just glad she has told them all about it.

They all go back to Naomi's room.
'Now you can see what frightened you,' says Auntie Julie.
'It's the shadow of that tree moving in the wind.'
Naomi can see that now,
but soon she'll be on her own again.
And she will still be afraid.
And there is nothing she can do about it.
The fear just comes all by itself.

'I think you're very brave,' says Auntie Julie.
'Me?' asks Naomi in surprise.
'Yes, you,' smiles her auntie. 'You have to be
very brave to admit that you're scared.'
Naomi had never thought about that.
'Now let's all go to bed,' says Auntie Julie.
'Could you leave the light on?' asks Naomi.
'Of course. It's the best way to keep ghosts away!'

The next morning, Auntie Julie has a good idea.
'Draw me some of the monsters you saw,' she says.
So Naomi and her cousin start to draw.
Soon they have drawn pages of monsters.
But - none of them are frightening.
They just look funny. Naomi thinks:
'If these are the monsters that visit me tonight,
I think I shall just laugh at them.'

'Come on,' says Naomi.
'Let's go and show these monsters to your mum.'
'Um, you go, I'll come in a minute.'
Caroline is staring at something
and looking worried.
Naomi spots a tiny spider on the end of its thread.
Is her brave cousin scared of a such a tiny creature?

Naomi picks up the spider.
'What are you doing?' cries Caroline.
'I'm putting it outside. Can you open the window?'
Caroline jumps aside as Naomi carries the spider past her.
'So, not afraid of anything, eh?' laughs Naomi.
'Well,' Caroline mutters, and shrugs her shoulders.
And her face slowly goes red. Very red.